Dear Parents and Educators,

Welcome to Penguin Young Readers! As parents and educators, you know that each child develops at his or her own pace—in terms of speech, critical thinking, and, of course, reading. Penguin Young Readers recognizes this fact. As a result, each Penguin Young Readers book is assigned a traditional easy-to-read level (1–4) as well as a Guided Reading Level (A–P). Both of these systems will help you choose the right book for your child. Please refer to the back of each book for specific leveling information. Penguin Young Readers features esteemed authors and illustrators, stories about favorite characters, fascinating nonfiction, and more!

Angelina Ballerina™
Angelina at Ballet Camp

LEVEL **2**

GUIDED READING LEVEL **I**

This book is perfect for a **Progressing Reader** who:
- can figure out unknown words by using picture and context clues;
- can recognize beginning, middle, and ending sounds;
- can make and confirm predictions about what will happen in the text; and
- can distinguish between fiction and nonfiction.

Here are some **activities** you can do during and after reading this book:
- Adding *ing* to Words: Here are three rules to use when adding *ing* to words: 1) If a word ends with a vowel and then a consonant, repeat the consonant before adding *ing*: sit/sitting. 2) If a word ends with an *e*, delete it before adding *ing*: give/giving. 3) If a word ends with two vowels and then a consonant, just add *ing*: clean/cleaning. Find the *ing* words in the story. On a separate sheet of paper, write the word and the root word next to it.
- Make Connections: In this story, Angelina has ~ ballet camp. She misses her teacher and ƒ class. But the next day, she makes new frie better. Have you ever tried something new you overcome your fear?

Remember, sharing the love of reading with a child is the best gift you can give!

—Bonnie Bader, EdM
   Penguin Young Readers program

*Penguin Young Readers are leveled by independent reviewers applying the standards developed by Irene Fountas and Gay Su Pinnell in *Matching Books to Readers: Using Leveled Books in Guided Reading*, Heinemann, 1999.

HiT entertainment

PENGUIN YOUNG READERS
Published by the Penguin Group
Penguin Group (USA) LLC, 375 Hudson Street, New York, New York 10014, USA

USA | Canada | UK | Ireland | Australia | New Zealand | India | South Africa | China

penguin.com
A Penguin Random House Company

Angelina Ballerina (Classic) © 2015 Helen Craig Ltd and Katharine Holabird. The Angelina Ballerina name and character and the dancing Angelina logo are trademarks of HIT Entertainment Limited, Katharine Holabird, and Helen Craig. Used under license by Penguin Young Readers Group. HIT and the HIT logo are trademarks of HIT Entertainment Limited. All rights reserved.
Published by Penguin Young Readers,
an imprint of Penguin Group (USA) LLC, 345 Hudson Street, New York, New York 10014.
Manufactured in China.

ISBN 978-0-448-48705-2   10 9 8 7 6 5 4 3 2 1

Angelina at Ballet Camp

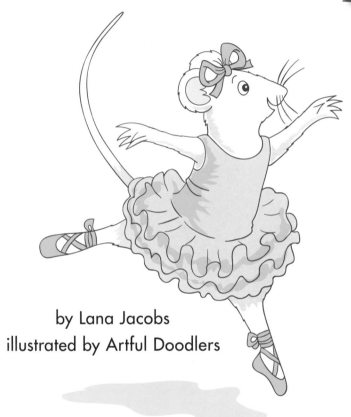

by Lana Jacobs
illustrated by Artful Doodlers

inspired by the classic children's book series by author
Katharine Holabird and illustrator Helen Craig

Penguin Young Readers
An Imprint of Penguin Group (USA) LLC

Angelina is happy.

The sun is shining.

It is hot outside.

It is summertime!

Angelina is going to ballet
camp this summer.
She wants to dance all day long
at camp.

At her camp, Angelina twirls.

She leaps.

She pirouettes.

But something is different about
ballet camp.

Where is Miss Lilly?

Where are Angelina's friends?

Angelina feels sad.

It is time to learn a new dance.

Angelina is having a hard time
learning the steps.

She trips during practice.

Oh no!

That night, Angelina tells her
mom, "I miss school."

"I miss Miss Lilly and all
my friends.
I don't want to go back
to ballet camp!"

Mrs. Mouseling gives Angelina a hug.

"I know it is scary to be in a new place," Mrs. Mouseling tells Angelina.

"But you get to make new friends and learn new things," she says. "Doing new things helps you grow.

Don't worry.

Tomorrow will be a better day."

In the morning, Angelina feels

better.

She is ready to go back to ballet
camp.

She smiles at the first mouseling
she sees.

"That is a beautiful dance,"
Angelina says to the mouseling.

"Can you teach me?" Angelina asks.

"Sure!" the mouseling says.

Angelina and her new friend
practice together.

Another mouseling joins in the

dance party.

Now Angelina is having fun!

After lunch, Angelina performs
her new dance routine for her
teacher.

"You worked hard to learn that routine," her teacher says. "I'm so proud of you for not giving up."

Angelina can't wait to show
Alice and Miss Lilly what she has
learned!

Angelina is happy that she stayed

at ballet camp.

She made new friends, and she is a better dancer now!

Suddenly, Angelina's best friend,

Alice, walks into the dance

studio.

What a great surprise!

"I'm joining camp, Angelina!"

Alice says.

The two friends hug each other tight.

Angelina can't wait to show Alice

around ballet camp.

They will dance together

every day.

This will be the best summer ever!